Fixed Up

by Joyce Voelker
illustrations by Sherry Neidigh

Mother said to me,
"You must work on your room today."

But I don't like fixing up my room.
So I'll play a game.
I'll find a home for all my things.

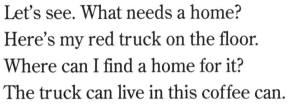

Let's see. What needs a home?
Here's my red truck on the floor.
Where can I find a home for it?
The truck can live in this coffee can.

But the coffee can
has fifteen white pebbles in it.
Where can I put the white pebbles?
I'll put the pebbles in this chest.
The chest will be a home for them.

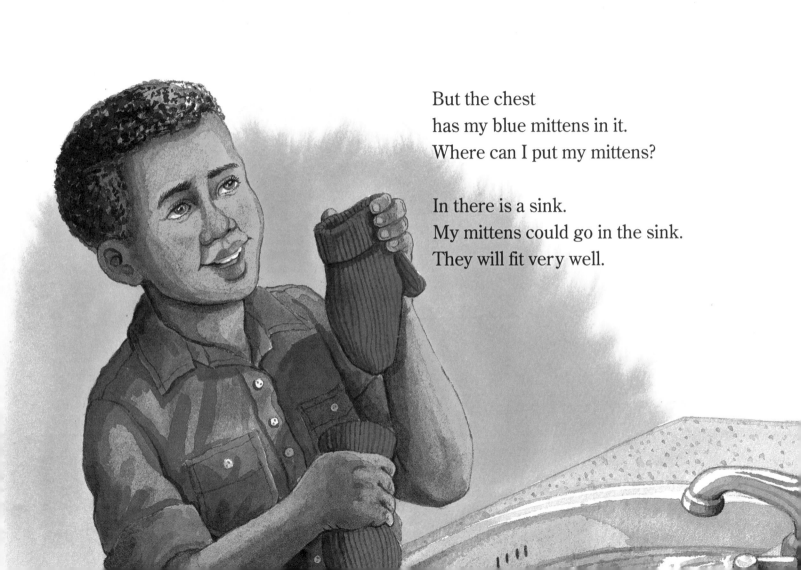

But the chest
has my blue mittens in it.
Where can I put my mittens?

In there is a sink.
My mittens could go in the sink.
They will fit very well.

But the sink has water in it.
Where shall I put the water?

I'll go get a big silver pot,
and I'll dip the water into it.
Mother will be glad that
my mittens didn't get wet.

But the big pot has green beans in it.
Where can I find a home for the beans?

Wait! This soap dish is green.
I will pile the green beans in the soap dish.
I'll pile them up high.

But the soap dish
has three little soaps in it.
They are yellow and they smell good.
They need a home. Where can I put them?

Couldn't I put the soaps in this shoe box?
The box will smell good too.

But the shoe box has shoes in it.
The soaps will fit
if I move these shoes.
Where can I put the shoes?
They can go in the fish tank.

But my pet frog lives in the fish tank.
Where can I find a home for a frog?
I think he would like to hop
into my sand pail.

What can I do with this orange?
I feel like a snack—
something sweet to eat.
Well, I got my job done,
so I'll peel this and eat it.

Mother! Come and see! I fixed up my room.